Collections
15 Strange Tales of Crime and Mystery
Entangled Realities (with Kim Antieau)
Labor Days
Miniatures
Mostly Invisible

Nonfiction
Kim and Mario Build a Labyrinth and So Can You
     (with Kim Antieau)

A Bestiary of Imaginary Species

Mario Milosevic

Green Snake
PUBLISHING

A Bestiary of Imaginary Species
by Mario Milosevic

ISBN: 978-1-949644-81-4

All cover and interior illustrations by
Mario Milosevic.

This book is a wholly artisanal work by the author, a sentient being. It was written and illustrated with no contributions from artificial intelligence.

The following entries originally appeared on Mario Milosevic's blog *Conditional Reality:* Chronofrond, Cumulatino, Erronion, Fire Leech, Human, Insulat, Knitter, Menamonium, Quooquoo, Radicker, Severlense, Skware, Tastick, Tomeater, and Wameker. The remainder are original to this volume.

Thanks to Kim Antieau and Don Price.

Published by Green Snake Publishing
www.greensnakepublishing.com

Contents

For all the imaginary beings
wherever they may be.

Introduction

Collections of descriptions of animals, both real and imagined, came to be called bestiaries and have been a part of literature for many centuries. They were originally meant to give moral guidance and sometimes offer a bit of satire. They eventually evolved into nature guides which are much more reliable records of the natural world.

Bestiaries also became a literary genre in their own right. Many authors have produced bestiaries of all kinds.

This bestiary highlights the what-might-have-been animals of the world. Think of it as a list of those creatures that were *not* the most likely to succeed.

Even so, they are worth remembering. They recall a time and place of abundant wonder when imagination ruled.

—Mario Milosevic

A Bestiary of Imaginary Species

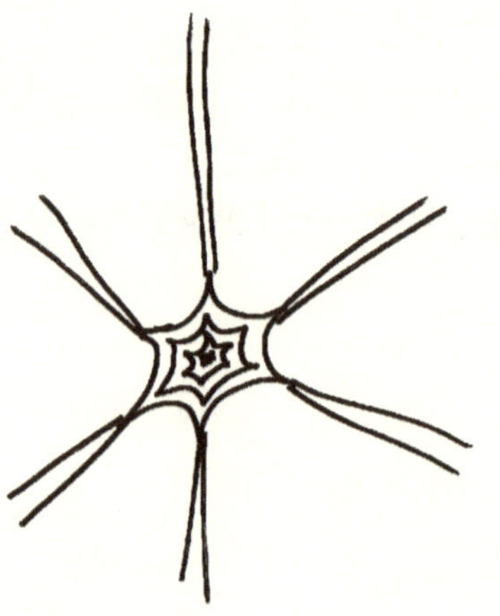

Adoka

Adoka were used for centuries as lighting. When placed in a dark environment, they draw in the darkness and transform it into shadowless spikes of light that radiate in slowly spinning spokes. Adoka normally live in ponds and swamps. They are often prey to frogs, herons, and other water creatures. People who have eaten adoka report they taste like lemons seasoned with a little salt. Their light is yellowish and soft. They reproduce only when radiating light. Male and female adoka mingle their spikes of light and remain entwined for several days. The female then lays a clutch of eggs and swims away. Few of the eggs hatch as they tend to glow and attract predators. Conservation efforts are underway to increase adoka numbers. This involves mostly covering up the eggs so they are not visible to other animals. Adoka feed on tadpoles and insects, though they shun those that display bioluminescence.

Amountalith

Amountalith live in the canopies of very tall trees where they feed on hummingbirds that mistake them for flowers. Amountalith resemble branches bearing flute-like blossoms. These appendages harbor a potent poison instead of nectar. The hummingbirds dip their beaks into the poison and are immediately paralyzed. The amountalith then feeds on the feathers of the hummingbird, letting the rest of the body fall to the ground. Amountalith were first described in the rainforests of Central America, but related species have since been found throughout the Americas in tall trees of all kinds. Amountalith are very shy and depend on their resemblance to branches for their survival. They are very hard to detect. Researchers who gather specimens report that they smell good enough to eat. However, those that do consume them endure vomiting and diarrhea that can last for weeks.

Ampouly

The ampouly haunts the dreams of many surgeons, ever since it was first documented during a liver transplant procedure at a hospital in Kenya in the 1980s. The surgeon noticed the creature cringing in a pool of blood near the newly installed liver. She thought it must be some tissue that she could attend to once her main task was complete, but this did not prove to be the case. The ampouly darted from its lair and wrapped itself around her scalpel, then quickly crawled up her arm and under her sleeve. She stopped the operation to retrieve the creature. Once she was able to grasp it, she held it between thumb and forefinger and stared at it. The ampouly stared back. Unfortunately, it had injured itself on the scalpel and in a few seconds it bled out and expired. Since then, many ampouly have been found in patients. They invariably give surgeons the willies.

Antejaq

Antejaqs have no ancestors in the tree of life. They appear to have been created from the head of a jackrabbit and the body of a deer. These creatures spend much of their time trampling through gift shops in the American West where they tear down instances of jackalopes. This has led many biologists to theorize that the antejaq has a streak of jealousy in its psyche. Others dispute this. Gift shop operators have learned to leave flowerpots planted with grass outside their places of business as a distraction. This does not always work, and antejaqs have been known to crash through windows to get at the offending jackalopes. Antejaqs are solitary creatures. They sometimes appear on highways where they will stand and face oncoming cars and snarl at them. Some motorists report driving right through the antejaqs as though they are ghosts. This phenomenon has not been independently confirmed.

Arbim

Arbim resemble folded up umbrellas when conditions are dry. At such times they tend to remain in their lairs, curled up with others of their tribe and hidden from the sun. When rains come, the arbim emerge and unfurl themselves, creating canopies over their squat bodies that deflect the rain to form a moat around them. Infant arbim find these circles of water, flock to them, and drink and drink and drink. They take in so much water that they resemble water balloons. They can also grow to twice their normal size during a good strong rain. Arbim are very shy creatures. They do not make good pets, though people have used them as living umbrellas. This fad flourished in the mid-nineteenth century, especially in areas prone to monsoons. Most governments have outlawed the practice as being inhumane. A thriving underground market in arbim, however, still exists.

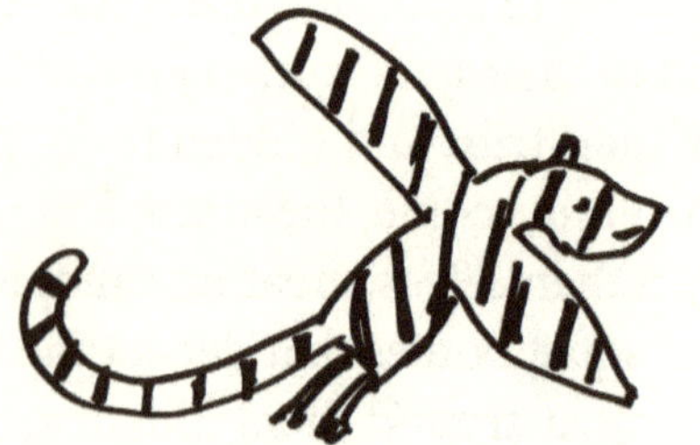

Basheliwik

Basheliwik were first recorded over cassava crops in Thailand. Biologists captured a few of these flying tigers and were immediately lulled into a state of torpor simply by being in the presence of their soft fur and purring sounds. Basheliwik are welcomed wherever they are found. They often scare away birds that would consume crops, and in the evening they sometimes land near houses and peer inside. Most locals are charmed by this behavior. Basheliwik do not build nests. Birds appear to be discomfited by the presence of any basheliwik and will sometimes peck at them on the wing. When flying, basheliwik do not purr. They mostly eat small rodents that favor the protection of the cassava leaves. Such protection is no match for the sharp eyesight of the basheliwik who sometimes have to horde piles of dead mice and rats because they are such easy targets for them.

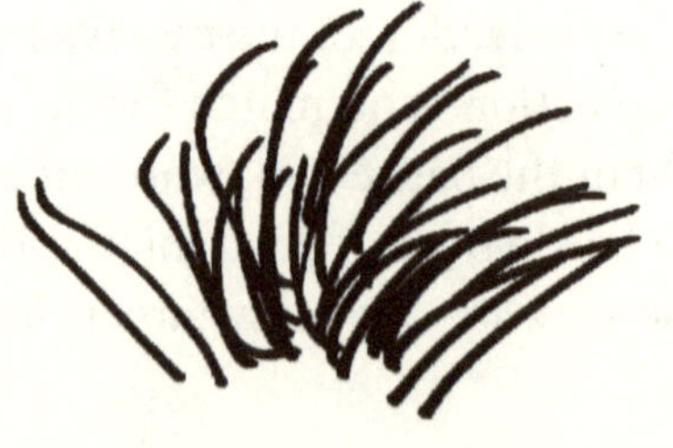

Bharstel

Bharstel resemble clumps of plant material. They have kept company with hair cutters for centuries and consume the clippings that fall to the floor from the heads of customers getting trims. When business is slow, hair professionals spend time conversing with bharstel. Though the creatures rarely answer, they have been known to prompt deep thoughts in the people tasked with making the hair of the general public fit for viewing by the rest of humanity. It is a heavy burden and the bharstel's abiding loyalty helps relieve some of the stress of this most sacred of tasks. Bharstel often wrap themselves around the legs of hair stylists. At night bharstel are known to occasionally consume hair coloring agents to change their own hue. They prefer bright neon colors and are especially partial to magenta.

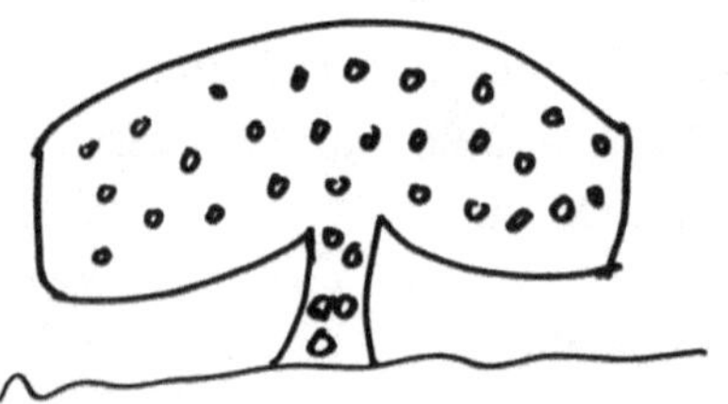

Canstin

Canstin emit an odor resembling a combination of carnivore feces, rotting flesh, and skunk. This effectively keeps them from being eaten as no creature will willingly spend any time in their vicinity. They are susceptible to rain and will melt when subjected to long periods of moisture. Solitary, since they are offensive even to other canstin, they spend their lives in one place, attaining nutrients from the ground beneath them. Sometimes mistaken for mushrooms, they have occasionally been harvested for food by desperate people nearing starvation. In such rare circumstances, the canstin will bleed out a sticky substance that increases the potency of its odor. Canstin reproduce parthenogenetically. Offspring crawl away within minutes of being born and will travel for days before realizing the odor they abhor comes from themselves. They then remain stationary for the balance of their days.

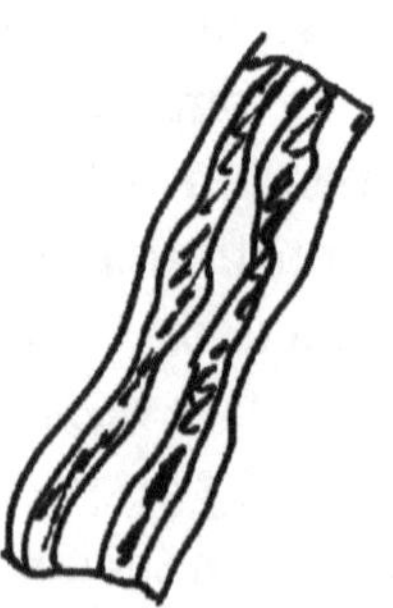

Cholrentin

Cholrentin inhabit mostly urban areas and can be found wherever populations exceed a density of about ten thousand people per square mile. Their numbers have exploded in the last hundred years or so. Cholrentin may be described as a network of muscle fibers. They don't appear to have a brain or nervous system. Cholrentin have been domesticated for centuries and trained to wrap themselves around human limbs for the purpose of aiding in locomotion. Some people develop life-long relationships with their cholrentin and experience significant bouts of depression when their cholrentin dies. Attempts have been made to remove cholrentin from urban settings and have them live in wilderness areas. These misguided enterprises invariably end in the death of the cholrentin.

Chronofrond

The chronofrond was discovered by a hiker who stopped along a trail and bent down to pick up what looked like a large leaf stuck in the mud. The "leaf" was actually the flat body of an animal. As she grasped the stem, the animal oozed away from her. Subsequent investigations revealed the chronofrond behaved like a rudimentary sundial. The stem-like appendage cast a deep red shadow onto its body. The chronofrond lived in a small and secluded area; however, a craze soon developed for chronofronds. People displayed them as exotic timepieces. Chronofronds were harvested to extinction. Some preserved specimens can still be found at clock repair shops.

Chynderskavich

The first recorded encounter with chynderskavich occurred in the northern reaches of Siberia where Russian miners in the late eighteenth century found them in nests around wild summer wheat. Their wide eyes and heart-shaped heads proved irresistible. The miners adopted them as pets and named them for the miner who first saw them. Soon after that, the miners discovered chynderskavich urine contained high concentrations of alcohol. Once they got over their revulsion, they took to drinking the urine with gusto. Their resultant drunken state made their working lives much more endurable. They took chynderskavich home with them and the creatures enjoyed wide acceptance for many years. Today only a few remain and are highly prized. The animals are very shy and rarely mate in captivity. No one who owns one wants to let them go, so they are likely destined to eventually die out.

Cradnasin

Cradnasin are considered pests by most real estate agents and artists by many creative types. They enter a subdivision and take the form of houses in the area. They mimic buildings so well that residents are fooled into thinking the cradnasin bodies are their actual homes. Removal is a time consuming and expensive proposition as cradnasin put down strong foundations that are difficult to break. They are thought to have originated in the Arctic and from there spread to most of the northern hemisphere. Cradnasin are completely benign. No cradnasin has every harmed a human. Some communities have welcomed them, creating entire towns of cradnasin homes. No one lives in them. They are there for the peace and solace they bring. Cradnasin move on after a decade or so. They have been observed crawling into the sea. No one knows what happens to them after that.

Cumulatino

Cumulatinos resemble jellyfish but live in clouds. They have little contact with humans although they have been observed in fog banks and sometimes get tangled up in airplane propellers. Two centuries ago a ballooning expedition by an Italian explorer collected samples of cumulatino which he kept in a humid room in Venice for several years and where they appeared to thrive on the humidity. The cumulatinos were a local sensation. Visitors stood in the room while the cumulatinos slid over their faces and outstretched hands. Many returned to the room repeatedly and said the cumulatinos felt like the caresses of lovers.

Deru

Deru were a vogue animal for a few years in nineteenth century Europe. Spanish visitors to Africa discovered them in the dunes of the Sahara. At first the creatures were aloof, but eventually they were drawn to the aromatic food the Spaniards had brought with them. Deru are small, no larger than a mouse. The explorers collected a few of the creatures and brought them back to Barcelona. They were prized for their long whiskers which would grow back after being plucked for the purpose of making artist brushes. The Deru reproduced rapidly and found homes across the continent. This did not last. People discovered they could no longer trust their family members if a deru was present. The deru affected the brains and personalities of their owners. This led to many arguments and abuse among the humans until the deru were removed and destroyed.

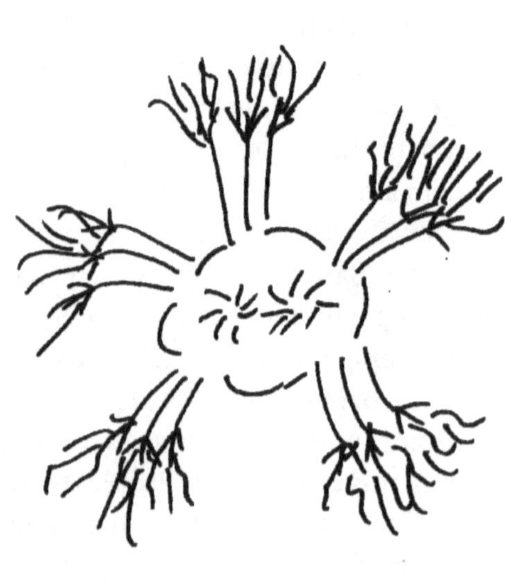

Dolpexa

Dolpexa are urchin-like creatures that spend most of their lives in the ocean. They are long-lived, with some individuals confirmed to be over two hundred years old. Near the end of their life cycles dolpexa migrate to tide pools where they remain for a year or two before undergoing a rapid increase in internal pressure resulting in an explosion that sends their organic matter bursting in all directions. This spectacle has been observed for thousands of years. Biologists theorize the explosions "seed" the water with their sperm and eggs which are then eaten by other sea creatures and excreted onto the ocean floor. The trip through the digestive system triggers the dolpexa's reproductive process. Dolpexa are warm to the touch. Certain ancient people regarded them as emissaries from the center of the Earth. More recently, some Mediterranean cultures have dubbed them "blood grenades."

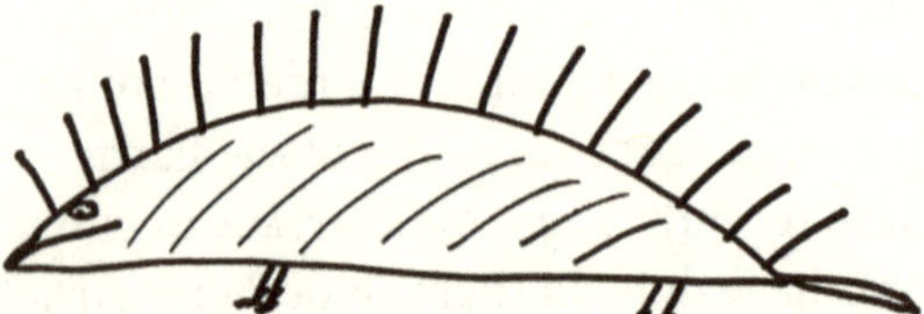

Eluhia

Eluhia were native to some south Pacific islands where generations of islanders broke off their spines and inserted the tips into their arms. A substance that induced hallucinations poured out of the spines resulting in several days of eerie visions. Eluhia were revered and protected for centuries. When Portugal began plying the oceans, their sailors encountered eluhia, pricked themselves with the spines, and were so enamored of the resulting visions that they gathered as many eluhia as they could find and took them back to Europe. The remaining eluhia on the islands died out due to loneliness. Native peoples there still harbor resentment toward the Portuguese for causing their extinction. Eluhia taken to Europe could not adapt to conditions there and all expired within a few months. Sailors saved the spines and rationed them to get high, but these too ran out. Eluhia are mourned to this day.

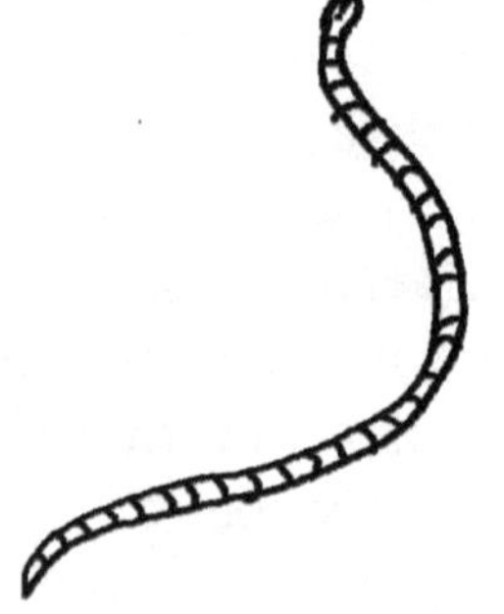

Emardita

Emardita have long been used for weight control. Ancient Sumerians wrote of the worm, as did physicians working during the Yin dynasty in China. Those seeking an effortless means of losing weight would swallow one of the worms which would then get to work consuming the person's fat. This would go on for as long as the person wanted. When they reached their preferred size, they swallowed another emardita. The two creatures would find each other and invariably fight to the death, presumably over the fat of the swallower. This method of weight loss went out of favor for centuries but was revived in nineteenth century North America and flourishes in small communities to this day. People who raise emardita report that the creatures are strangely soothing, emitting a low frequency humming that lulls listeners into a peaceful and reverent state conducive to deep sleep.

Eredeev

Eredeev routinely expel their eyes, which then fly around on their own. Usually they return to their owners, but when they don't the eredeev generates a new pair of eyes, a process that consumes all its energy so that it performs this regeneration in a state of torpor. This is when it is most vulnerable to predators but not to worry. They are poisonous to most creatures and are rarely eaten or maimed. The eyes are sometimes mistaken for animals in their own right. They are very swift, moving by the flapping of thin membranes that act as wings. These membranes retract into the eyeball when installed in the eye sockets of the eredeev. No one knows why the eyeballs fly about on their own. Theories include recognizance, weariness of the host, collecting nutrients from the air, and the exhilaration of flight. None of these have been proven to be true.

Erronion

The erronion is a small songbird, native to Oregon and Washington, with two sharp horns growing out of its skull. The horns, thin and hollow, are a vivid and lustrous red in the male and a muted green in the female. Early European invaders called the erronion "the devil's bird" and avoided it as much as possible. Its song is a repeating liquid cascade of nine notes: *twee lee klee tu thwp thwp thwp traaaaaaa la*. Rock art images of erronion birds are common throughout its range. Bears follow flocks of them to find fields of ripe berries to feed on.

Ezzan

Ezzan live in the underbrush in and around boreal forests. They resemble seed pods with feathery hairs, but harbor numerous sharp teeth which they keep hidden most of the time. When eaten whole by snakes, they feign dormancy within the snake's body. Their tough outer shells prevent them from being digested. After a few days they eat their way out of the snake's body. The snake invariably dies. The ezzan, on the other hand, consume the remainder of the snake and go on to be swallowed by other snakes, only to eat their way out of each one. Ezzan are symbols of rebirth and often figure in folktales where they are sometimes identified as members of the walking dead tribe. In some of these tales they are depicted as resourceful heroes. In others, they play the role of grotesque horror. In all legends they are accorded deep respect.

Fire Leech

Adult fire leeches live in the windpipes and on the tongues of dragons. They remain dormant in forests in their infancy, experience rapid and dramatic growth spurts during forest fires, then migrate to the respiratory systems of dragons. Knights discovered them crawling on the ground after dragon beheadings. Fire leeches have tough outer shells with a high mineral content. They live on flames and require, at minimum, a warm environment. They are shy creatures, preferring darkness when available. Fire leeches can sometimes be found clustered around the hot coals of barbecues. They are harmless to humans but make poor pets.

Flierfie

This insect does not sting; instead it burns. As it alights on a body, it emits a flame from its mouth that scorches the skin. This is an effective form of defense, since people generally retreat from the area, not wanting to be burned again. Some folks, however, cultivate the burns and apply flierfies to their skin repeatedly to make intricate patterns that rival the artistry of the very best tattoos. Researchers believe the flierfies consume coal dust to produce their flames, however this has not been confirmed. Flierfies figure in many mythologies from cold climates. They are often depicted in folktales as light bearers, idea generators, and bringers of knowledge.

Fodonsilf

Fodonsilf reproduce very rapidly with a new generation born every month or so. This is fortunate for the survival of the species since their only food source is other fodonsilf. Biologists have attempted to feed fodonsilf other foods, but in every case these alternative nutrients have been soundly rejected, even when refusal led to their demise. Their lives are a race against death in an endless balance between sex and food. Meals generally occur after mating, though reproduction is not ensured in all cases, since the female is as likely to be eaten as the male. Surviving females lay eggs, usually buried in beach sand. They hatch after about three weeks, which means most fodonsilf spend more time as an egg than as a hatched creature. Fodonsilf mating and feeding displays are operatic. Many cultures have legends about their antics. None end happily.

Gangliroot

Centuries ago some early tinkerers in the dark arts thought to graft a tree onto the head of a rabbit. The result was a creature with a plodding gait and a patient perspective on life. The roots of the tree went deep into its brain and mingled with the neurons there until they were so entangled that it would be impossible to separate them. Thus the creature came to think of itself as a tree. All instances of this species retreated to an island off the coast of Japan and were forgotten for many years until an expedition of naturalists arrived, saw them, and named them gangliroots. These creatures are remarkably docile and friendly. All they want to do is offer shade and protection. Their bark is just as benign as their bite.

Gindachert

Gindacherts swallow eggs and incubate them until the birds hatch. The gindachert has only kindness in its heart. It never digests the birds. In certain areas mating pairs welcome the gindachert to their nests knowing their offspring will be safe. Gindachert always allow the hatchlings to crawl out of its stomach, up its throat, and out into the world. In exchange, the gindachert derives nutrients from the shells of the eggs. Gindachert can be found in hot climates wherever swamps are prevalent. When incubating eggs, they turn a distinctive shade of orange. At other times they are a drab blue. Gindachert have been harvested for food by many cultures. They are said to taste like pork. Other cultures are taught to never touch them and to leave them to their activities. These precepts have lead to many discussions regarding the ethics of consumption. Gindachert never participate in any of these debates.

Greewen

These creatures crawl into the ear canals where they act as natural hearing aids, amplifying any sounds they encounter. Those infested with greewen invariably seek relief from their effects since the apparent volume of the sound is overwhelming. Greewen take nourishment from the ear wax of their hosts and emerge from the ear canal only to mate, usually in the host's hair. This is the most opportune time to get rid of them. Some people actually befriend their greewen, though such individuals are rare. Greewen were first observed in the elaborate hair decorations of banana plantation workers in Costa Rica. This led some biologists to suggest they came from banana plants, though this has not been confirmed. Greewen often outlive their hosts. They can sometimes be found in the caskets of the deceased, where they wander around in a daze.

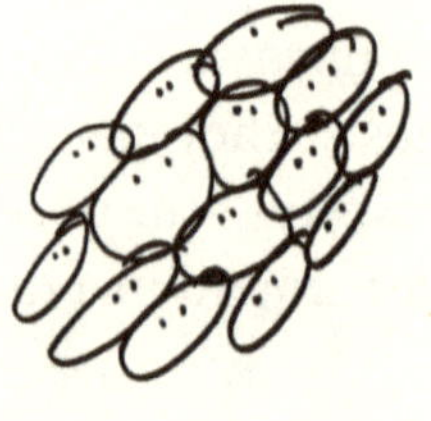

Grudagrot

The grudagrot looks like an ordinary pile of gravel until it is disturbed by a passing creature. This prompts the appendages that resemble small smooth rocks to rise up and wrap themselves around the offending animal's ankle. It's nothing to be concerned about. Grudagrots don't attack. Instead they hug. They are usually found in gravel pits where they can generally remain unseen and unnoticed. They were once thought to be a species of mushroom until researchers observed their movements which are decidedly unlike any other mycelium. Grudagrots reproduce by parthenogenesis, each appendage breaking off in the spring to roll away and begin growing appendages of its own. It feeds on algae and other water-borne microorganisms, but can go years without eating, which makes it particularly well-adapted to desert climates. Grudagrots emit tumbling sounds that can be very soothing.

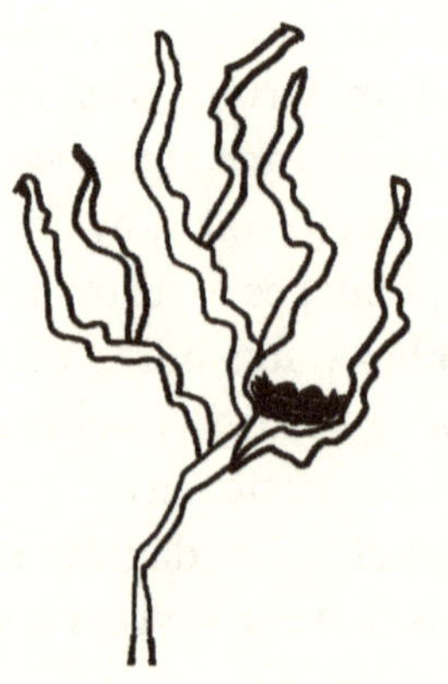

Hangasy

Hangasy possess limbs that look like the branches of dead trees. They fool birds into building nests on them. Hangasy don't eat birds or their eggs. Instead they wait for the eggs to hatch and the hatchlings to grow up and fly away. They then consume the nests. Hangasy live on only a couple of nests a year. Biologists believe the hangasy derive nourishment from the droppings that the parent bird leaves in the nest. Some hangasy have been shown to be over a thousand years old. They grow very slowly which fooled many people into believing they were the snags they resemble. They appear to have originated in Thailand where they lived in vast groups comprising thousands of individuals. A volcanic eruption in the area millions of years ago prompted them to migrate north and west to Bangladesh where most existing individuals of the species live today.

Hidey Do

Astronomers observed several anomalies in the signals emanating from the black hole at the center of our galaxy. None of them could account for the radically altered pulsations or the increase in mass consumption. After many months of head-scratching they consulted an animal biologist who examined the data and immediately recognized the anomalies as signs of a living creature. She found evidence of all the basics of life: movement (it vibrated); reproduction (it had created a mini black hole); sensitivity (it detected an increase in solar masses in its immediate vicinity); excretion (it radiated sub atomic particles); nutrition (it swallowed cosmic dust with a voracious appetite); respiration (it breathed in and out); and growth (it's diameter was increasing). She named it hidey do and began planning an expedition to meet it.

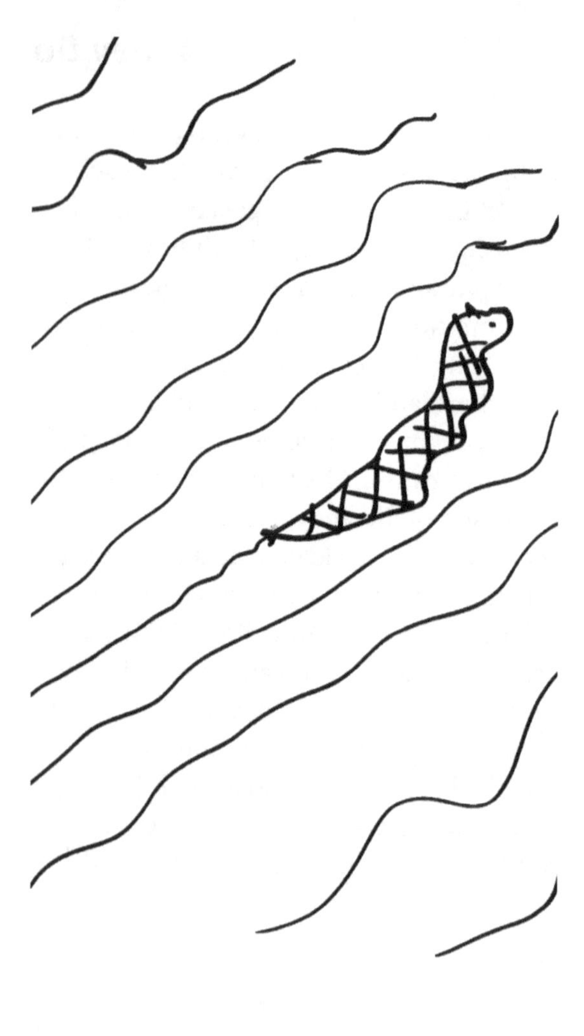

Hiiwam

Georgia O'Keeffe and Frida Kahlo are rumored to have included some of these slug-like creatures in their art supplies. Pablo Picasso, not to be outdone, famously claimed to own several of his own. None of these reports have ever been confirmed, but it is undeniable that hiiwams can assist in creating images. They exude pigmented slime as they meander across a canvas. Artists who want to work with them can control their paths with certain baits that will alter the line of their journey or change the hue of their trail. Hiiwams were first documented in Australia where they were found in great colonies that produced iridescent tableaus on the surfaces of lakes. They were exported around the world as curiosities. Contemporary artists who wish to utilize them must resort to the shadow economy since the international community made trade in them illegal.

Human

The most amusing aspect of this hilarious species is that most of its members do not regard themselves as imaginary. But humans are well known deniers of reality. They constantly build things which fall down. They often prefer lies to truth and stories to history. Humans cling to variations of a fantastic legend which depicts them as being made by supernatural beings. This view colors every aspect of their lives. They believe their raw material is the atoms of stars. Humans see worlds in mirages and find joy in reproduction. This volume takes inspiration from their audacious spirit and insistent misperceptions.

Huppen

These snail-like creatures move about by hitching rides on the tops of tortoises. They possess perfectly functional lobes, but prefer not to use them for locomotion. Zoologists have not determined why this is so. Occasionally a huppen will slip off its host tortoise. In most cases the tortoise will then halt and wait for the huppen to crawl back up on the shell. This can take several minutes but the tortoises don't care. They have infinite patience. Huppens emit a dull glow at night that seems to aid the tortoise in navigation. During daylight hours huppens will often sing a song that can evoke a feeling of melancholy in those who hear it. When Charles Darwin first observed them on the backs of turtles near Bahía Blanca in Argentina, he called them the sad stars. The name did not stick.

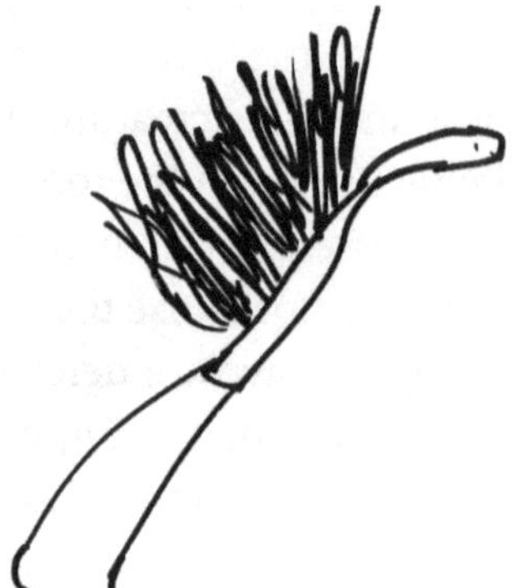

Icarlepos

Aristotle, among his many errors, once wrote that the icarlepos incubated in acorns. It was not until the seventeenth century that the truth was uncovered. A Swedish naturalist demonstrated that icarleposes begin life as eggs very similar to acorns, which allows them to be camouflaged on oak trees. When they hatch, invariably at night, they display plant fibers in place of feathers. All icarleposes are blind. They take to the air quickly and live aloft for the rest of their days, eating insects and never alighting on any perch ever again. When the sun dries out their wings, they drop from the sky. Heaps of dead icarleposes can often be seen in grassy fields at the height of summer. They exude a richly sweet and nutty fragrance as they decay. Carrion eaters carry their eggs to oak trees where the next generation begins its life cycle.

Imps Eider

In certain parts of northern British Columbia, children are tattooed before their first birthdays. Families that observe this ritual are generally shunned and have retreated to remote forest villages. Designs applied to the skin of such children generally involve nature themes such as birds or bears. Children who undergo such treatment report the presence of imps eiders usually around their tenth birthday. These creatures live in the tattoos and consume the ink. They cause hallucinations in the owner of the tattoo and over time will transform the image into colors much brighter than the original. Imps eiders resemble fleas with trunks. They move slowly, traversing a typical tattoo over the course of years. They cause itching, prompting some tattooed people to scratch at them. They are, however, extremely tenacious and cannot be removed. Ever.

Insulat

The insulat's unique life cycle begins in late summer when insulat shrubs produce tiny bundles of dark green fibers on their branches. These rapidly grow into cocoons which are chewed from the inside by the infant insulat worms. As the insulat consumes the cocoon it grows wings. The insulat takes to the air, navigating one long flight during which it will almost certainly be eaten by a bird. Those very few insulats that survive crawl into the ground where they die. In the spring their wings transform into shoots, which grow into shrubs, which produce bundles of dark green fiber.

Jil were first observed by early manufacturers of light bulbs. The worm-like creatures crawled into the bulbs and replaced the filaments with their own bodies. They gave off a softer and more pleasing light, but they only survived a short time and became a nuisance instead of an asset. Heaps of dead jil accumulated in the bulbs and they required an army of workers to clear them out. Little is known of their life cycle. Zoologists speculate that they incubate in the wires of the power grid. Today very few survive, although they can still occasionally be found in incandescent bulbs. Jil never make a sound. They live and die in complete silence, their only mark on the world is a bit of bright light, which effectively becomes their swan song.

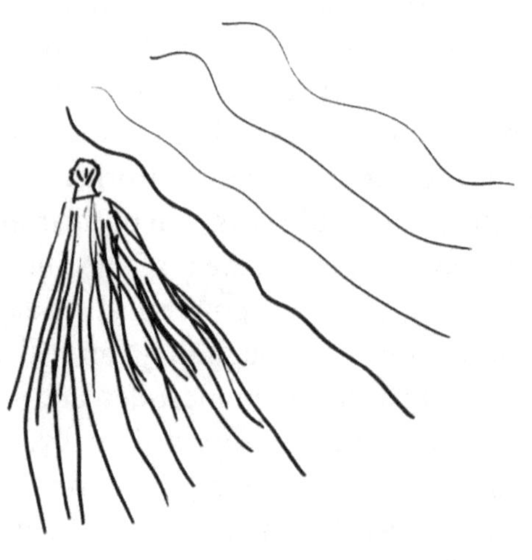

Jorah

Jorah are churned from the ocean and get washed up onto beaches on the northern coast of Australia where they resemble exotic shells that can exceed several feet in diameter. As the sun heats their crusty exteriors, they begin to metabolize their tissue into long strands of hair which unnervingly crawl along the sand, dip beneath the surface, and begin transforming the shoreline into a kind of hairscape. The original shell shrinks to the size of an orange. Jorah were once thought to be poisonous because birds, especially seagulls, choked on the hair. The hair, in fact, holds medicinal properties, including the ability to disinfect cuts when wrapped tightly around a wound. This benefit prompted First Peoples there to protect the jorah. Today jorah live free on several beaches reserved for them. Visitors are required to remove their shoes when treading on jorah land.

Kamori

Kamori are created when paper mills toss out the trimmings cut from the reams. The wind catches some of these scraps and takes them up up into the atmosphere where they are folded, origami-like, into creatures. Most of them don't survive, but some land on their feet and prowl neighborhoods in search of food. They eat mostly wasp nests when they can find them. If those are not at hand, they will eat birch bark and if that isn't available, they will resort to other tree barks or dried leaves. Kamori often end up in courtyards where the residents come out to greet them. The kamori welcome this attention and often eat tissue paper offered to them. They have been known to fold themselves up and spend the night but are usually gone before sunrise. They leave creases in the ground wherever they go.

Icebergs and glaciers have been home to karmas for centuries. They are made of ice and are so well camouflaged in the vicinity of large ice formations that they will remain undiscovered for at least 20 years, probably not until all the ice caps melt due to climate change. In the meantime, we can indulge our predilection for unfounded speculation by saying that karmas will be found to have the shape of donuts glazed with frost. They will be named for the etymological roots of hard (kar) and water (ma). They will present scientists with career-making puzzles about the nature of the strange markings on their surface. There will be a race to document their life cycle before most of them melt into the ocean. A few will be preserved in laboratory freezers, but those too will expire when the power grid permanently fails, some time before the beginning of the twenty-second century.

Knitter

The knitter, a close relative of the spider, fashions structures from human hair that can resemble the familiar design of a spider's web but more often mimics the entwining architecture of pigtails. Knitters are native to equatorial regions where ancient peoples placed them in their hair to make tight braids. The knitter has various shapes of claws on the ends of its forelegs which it uses to manipulate strands of hair. Knitters often fall into a frenzy of wild thrashing when constructing their hair designs. Their young sometimes get tangled up in the braids. They harden there like tiny decorative beads.

Kuzine

Kuzine are born with an elaborate network of stringy material in their hearts. They can pluck these strings using their brain power alone. Kuzine also possess the ability to memorize any piece of music in an instant. They then replay the melody using the strings in their hearts. Kuzine have been put to use as musical instruments by cultures across the globe and are invariably a source of much wonder and speculation to any who encounter one. They reproduce only rarely and must survive a long childhood and adolescence before they become adept at mimicking music. If left on their own, they copy bird songs and coyote howls. People become addicted to their sounds. Many have been known to give up their jobs, families, and even food just to track downa kuzine in the wild. When they find one, the music is enough to put them in a state of extended bliss that becomes a threat to their survival.

Lamithel

Some time in the distant past—estimates have ranged from 100 million to 200 million years ago—lamithels were abundant in the great plains of what would become North America. They were eaters of light, consuming whatever illumination came from the stars and the sun. This behavior plunged the area into darkness resulting in widespread plant and animal death and desertification of the area. Lamithel fossils indicate they used the light they ingested as incubating environments for their young. A massive volcanic eruption at the time blocked out the sun for many years, resulting in the complete eradication of all lamithels. Fossils of these tiny creatures are highly prized. Those with teeth intact are considered some of the most valuable fossils anywhere. There have been calls to resurrect the species. So far this urge has been resisted.

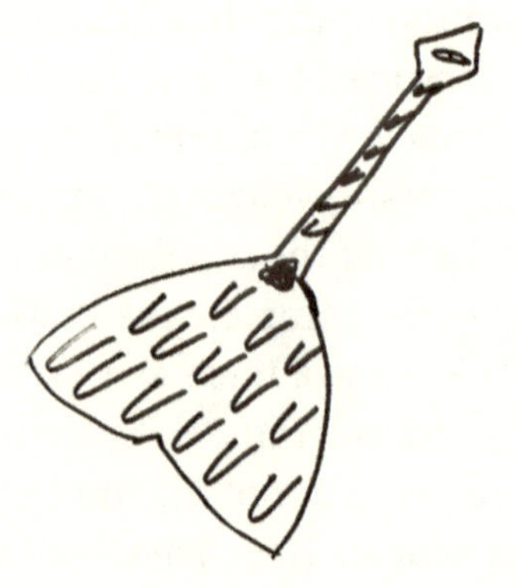

Laxeetix

The laxeetix makes its home in brackish ponds where it is mostly unseen. It is a strong swimmer and feeds mostly on tadpoles and water skimmers. It has inhabited North American waters for millions of years. Its one eye, on the end of a long stalk, is an unblinking searchlight always plowing forward and dragging its feathered body behind. Laxeetix emit a screeching call that is annoying to most humans, however beavers find it quite soothing. They will be lulled to sleep in the presence of screeching laxeetix. Followers of certain faiths burn the feathers of laxeetix and inhale the fumes to induce visions of flight. The laxeetix appear to be a descendant of a flying creature which flourished about ten million years ago. Laxeetix have hearts of stone, located at the base of the eye stalk. It is thought infant laxeetix capture their stones, though this has never been observed.

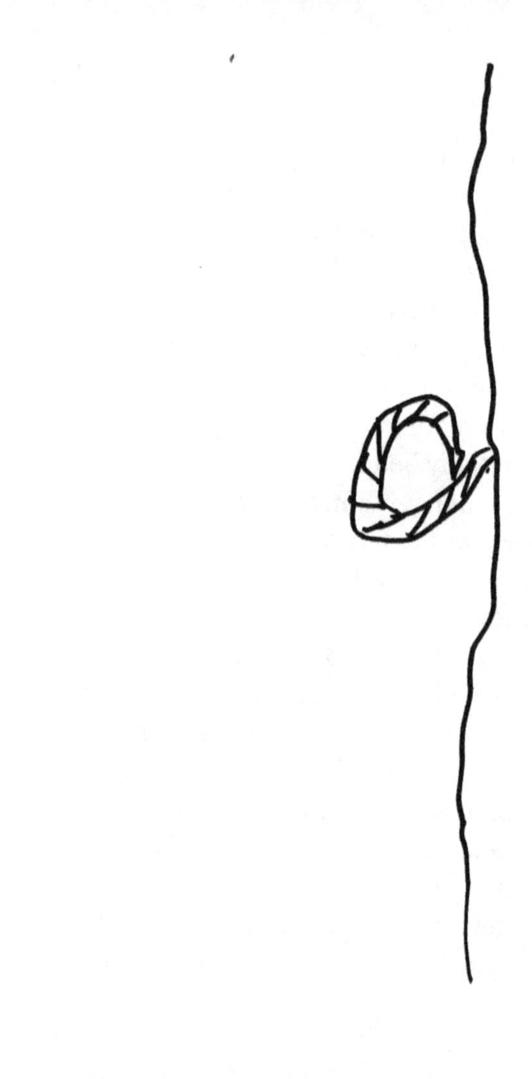

Lazouraché

Lazouraché live mostly in caves and will hibernate for years at a time. When first discovered in the Dordogne region of France, it was thought to be a fungus. It consists of many rope-like appendages that twist around and attach to rocks. Sometimes the ends of these appendages will display markings that resemble faces. Lazouraché occasionally leave their caves and venture out into the countryside. They generally remain unseen, oozing along in the grass. Hundreds of them will gather in the evening and entwine themselves into a knotted bundle. This sight usually unnerves anyone who encounters it. The lazouraché squirm, writhe, and emit piercing cries. They continue this behavior for several hours, then each lazouraché retreats to its cave for another few years. They eat bat droppings and have been observed strangling stray animals that accidentally venture into caves.

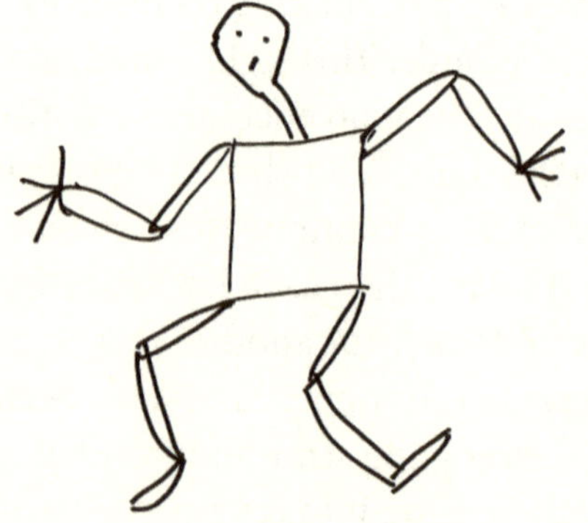

Loads Tone

All of a loads tone's bones are magnets due to a serious overabundance of iron in their diets. Each bone has a north pole and a south pole and they don't always match up so as to avoid repulsions. Consequently, they move in a herky-jerky fashion with their limbs askew, wobbly, and decidedly grotesque in appearance, very much like marionettes. Loads tones are often seen in wrecking yards where they can be observed tasting plastic and fiberglass parts of old vehicles which they then spit out with vehemence. Some have been recruited for military applications, but proved to be so contrary in nature that all such programs were terminated. Loads tones like to dig deep into the ground, some say in search of the magnetic core of the planet.

Lowaset

This creature spends its first few years as a more or less empty husk that resembles a dried out seed. Individual lowasets get distributed around the globe by winds which deposit them on trees where they then grow into a kind of crustacean that builds nests out of the leaves at its disposal. They stop growing when they are approximately two inches in diameter. Lowasets have many names, depending on the surrounding culture of their destination trees. In all instances, however, they are considered charming and quirky. They readily approach humans and will crawl all over them if given a chance. This behavior is completely harmless and has been shown to benefit those going through grief. In some parts of Tibet lowasets are given as gifts to families in which someone has died. Houses overrun with them are known to be places where healing begins.

Mandus

The mandus is all ears. It takes in sound and converts it to food, much like plants turn sunlight into nutrition. A mandus in a soundproofed room is a dead mandus within a short time. A mandus at a rock concert grows stronger, bigger, and more protective. Manduses have been in the historical record for centuries. Sumerian cuneiform tablets mention them. They are ubiquitous in many windy regions of the world and gravitate to tornadoes and hurricanes. They are solitary creatures but they are not shy. They like to display themselves on sandy ground and have been known to frequent beaches where they take in the sound of the surf hitting the shore. Their ears are prized trophies in many cultures. Necklaces composed of several mandus ears adorn the necks of countless people in ancient drawings. Such depictions make many people sad.

Mariole

The mariole is susceptible to the telepathic powers of bees. They cannot resist the call of the honey-makers, who lure them with silent thought harpoons. No one knows why the bees do this. They don't eat the marioles, or enslave them, or befriend them. Instead, the marioles drop out of clouds and get gummed up in the honey-combs of bee colonies, where they remain for the remainder of their days while the bees go about their business oblivious to their presence. Mariole were once thought to be spiders, but they have since been shown to be a species of frog. They seldom grow to be more than a quarter-inch across. Their two long thick antennae are thought to receive the mental emanations of the bees. Marioles detest honey. The bees, some biologists believe, find this highly amusing.

Menamonium

Menamoniums look like teddy bears and congregate at construction sites where they make cages from the building materials they find. They enter the cages and pose for passersby, who often reward them with bits of food. Authorities usually release them to the wild then destroy their cages. The menamoniums find their way back to the construction sites and rebuild their cages. Menamoniums have been called natural zoo creatures. They invite oohs and aahs. Kids are particularly susceptible to their charms and will want to take them home. Parents have learned to tell lies about how menamoniums like to eat children.

Mushoornie

Mushoornie are fiercely territorial. Clans of them will stake out territory in landfills and keep other scavengers at bay with their misshapen horns that emit a sound which can literally break bones. This usually occurs with other small mammals, but even some humans have experience fractured fingers and toes after sustained sonic attacks from these diminutive beasts. Mushoornie burrow under the debris of landfills and create extensive networks of tunnels and nests. They are found only in North America where their horns were once harvested for use as a food additive. When ground, it became a useful thickening agent in soups and stews and imparted a mild nutty flavor that many found irresistible. Mushoornie saw their numbers dwindling and undertook a generations-long campaign to make their horns taste of rotten meat. This stopped the hunt and saved the species.

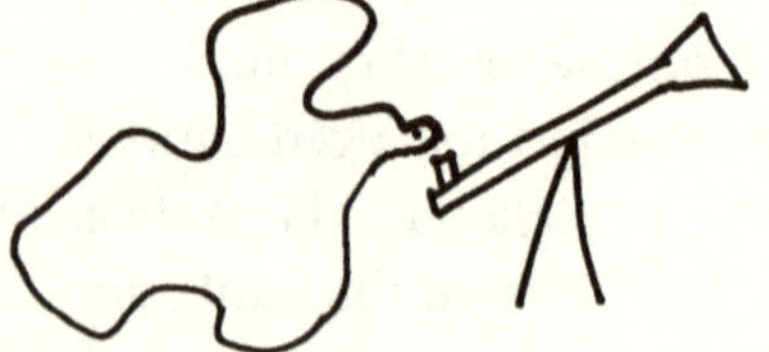

Myben

Myben are microscopic creatures first observed in the seventeenth century soon after microscopes became widely available. They moved like many other single-celled creatures, scurrying about here and there on a slide. Annabelle Power, an early and ardent advocate for the microscope, asserted that she saw a myben bent over a small instrument that resembled a telescope. She was ridiculed and banished to the dustheap of scientific history, even though she insisted on what she saw. It was not until centuries later that she was vindicated when a team of scientists, all female, documented exactly what Power had claimed. They found a group of myben rustling and vibrating near a tiny telescope. Annabelle Power was restored to the status of esteemed scientist. Today teams of scientists present portraits of Power to the myben telescopes to honor her pioneering work.

Nayhans

A few million years ago nayhans had horns made of keratin. They were fragile things and offered no protection from predators. Nayhans adopted venomous snakes to help them survive in their native grasslands. The snakes eventually merged with the nayhans and replaced their horns. Nayhans then became the most feared creatures anywhere as their enemies would be bitten by the snakes if they ever dared approach. This symbiotic relationship endured for many hundreds of thousands of years and nayhans grew to enormous size. The snakes kept pace, achieving impressive length. As the years passed, the snakes decided to strike out on their own. Nayhans quickly succumbed to predators and are now extinct. The snakes, however, thrived on their own and are feared by almost everyone who encounters them or even thinks about them.

Nefiltimen

Nefiltimen are distant relatives of the octopus. At some point in their evolution, their eight legs fused into four and they left the ocean to become land creatures. They lived on tall mountains, mostly in the Himalaya range, though individuals have been found on almost all tall ranges across the globe. They eat lichen and mushrooms and according to myth hold up the sky with their enormously long tentacles. They live an enormously long time and reproduce only sporadically. Locals have known about them for millennia and many trek up mountains to talk to them. Nefiltimen welcome visitors. They can converse for hours as a time, though the conversation almost invariably devolves into whining about their burden in life. They also sing with grace and beauty.

Norbhu

The norbhu is often mistaken for a robot since it is clad in stainless steel. However, this is just an armor it wears. Under all that metal is a living, breathing, misshapen, carbon-based creature prone to all the ailments that can befall any organic being. Norbhus spend a lot of time polishing their outer shells. Zoologists have presented competing ideas about where the metal comes from. The most prevalent theory is that norbhus scavenge the metal from dumps. Several sighting of norbhus near landfills lends support to this view, but it has not been verified. Norbhus like to click their metal pieces against each other. In some wilderness areas this clicking can be so loud and intrusive that other animals will run away from the source, leaving the norbhus alone and—some researchers believe—lonely. It is at those times that they get very interested in polishing their metal.

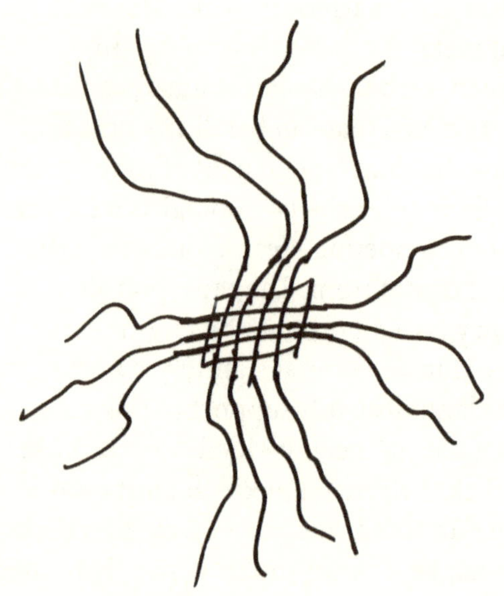

Oidari

Oidari were unknown until mirrors were first constructed from glass. They are thin and flat and live between the glass and the gilded surface behind. They are also transparent, but distort the images people see when they look into the mirror. Oidari contain a mild acid that etches lines into the mirror. These lines are conduits to the oidari world, which has never been visited by outsiders. Oidari reproduce in these channels and will spend their days refracting images through their bodies, subtly changing their color. Many people who see themselves in mirrors infected by oidari never allow themselves to be seen in public again. Instead, they become reclusive and antagonistic to any who dare to visit. The oidari are okay with this. They believe all creatures should be alone.

Oitevic

Oitevic are small, rarely exceeding a few millimeters in length. They begin life in the ice fields of the lunar south pole where they spend their days huddled against the cold. They survive only because their outer shells produce heat by the friction of individual plates rubbing against each other as the oitevic shiver and shake in a constant frenzy of dancing. This strategy's efficacy diminishes as oitevic age. Eventually they crawl out of their ice-lined craters where they encounter the energy of the sun, which lifts them off the lunar surface and sends them on a trajectory toward the Earth. The vast majority end up drowning in an ocean, usually the Pacific. Their dead husks are favored as food by whales.

Oporse

For centuries oporse lived only in the dreams of traumatized people. This did not stop the British government from attempting to release instances of oporse from the dreams of grieving women who had been made widows by the deaths of their soldier husbands in the early 1940s. The point was to employ the oporse as weapons in the war against Germany. The oporse resisted manifesting into the material world. They were eventually coaxed into doing so by hypnotizing the widows who were only too eager to release the oporse from their dreams. The oporse destroyed the sleep lab, then escaped and spent several weeks in and around London where they frightened children and cats. Eventually they were captured and destroyed. The widows reported a curious sensation of grief upon hearing the news. They experienced restless nights for the remainder of their years.

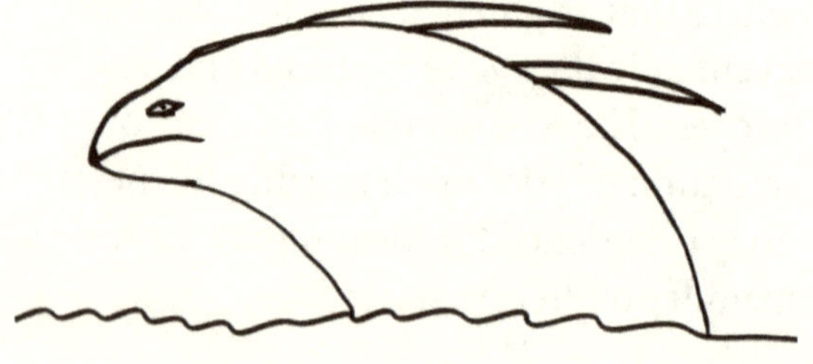

Owek

This creature is sighted about once a year in the Beagle Channel near the city of Ushuaia in the southern reaches of Argentina. Locals believe it to be the reincarnation of an inmate who died while trying to escape from the town prison in 1912. The inmate most likely perished in the channel south of the city. He was a known horse thief and horse lover. His body was never found. Owek are reclusive and timid. When approached by fishing vessels, they invariably turn and swim away. They are considered omens of good fortune as they represent a kind of return from death. Owek eat mostly seaweed but will occasionally attack and consume seals. They are ecstatic swimmers, splashing repeatedly when feeding and trail high waves as they ply the water. They also sing, releasing haunting melodies under full moons.

Peklin

Peklin resemble decayed pine cones to such an extent that biologists did not notice them until the 1890s when a group of hikers discovered an entire colony in the forests of northern California. Peklin look harmless but have lethal teeth that spring out when prey—in the form of butterflies or moths—fly near. Peklin employ these jaws to snatch the flying food right out of the air. Peklin have been known to hang on trees, but usually hunt on the ground. They live about a year or two, often not able to survive the winter. Nothing is known of their reproductive process. Peklin have inspired several songs and many paintings including *Peklin Nights* by Auntie Mika. Some people adopt them as pets, enjoying the macabre spectacle of watching flying creatures get pulled from the air. Several animal rights groups work to put a stop to this practice but it persists as a secret vice in many communities.

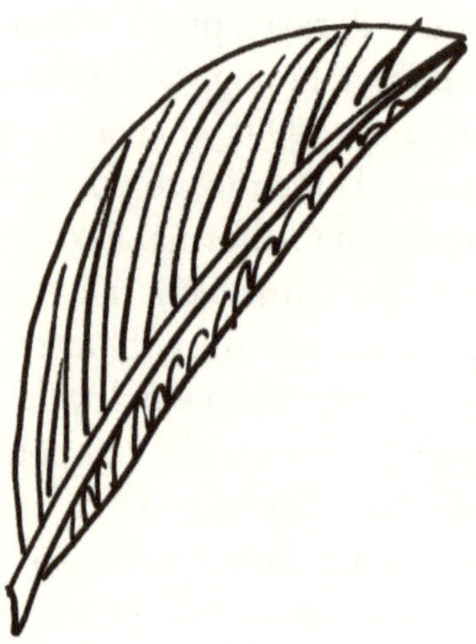

Pentena

Pentena take the form of feathers and attach themselves to the wings of birds where they perfectly blend it. For centuries biologists believed such creatures must exist, but none were actually observed until a girl in Ghana encountered one in the wings of a road kill vulture on the way home from school. She noted that one of the feathers was moving. It writhed and flopped about on the wing. She plucked it from the dead bird and brought it home to her mother, a biologist, who showed it her her colleagues. They all knew this was an important find and the girl became famous. Pentena move by catching the wind. They consume whatever nutrients they can find in dust and derive moisture from the air. They are the gentlest of creatures. The girl was allowed to keep the one she found. It remained her pet for many years, offering her most agreeable companionship.

Postoco

Divers near the town of Matara on the southern coast of Sri Lanka first observed this sea creature last century. They thought it was a squid tangled up in some seaweed, but quickly realized it was a squid-*like* creature with appendages resembling braided hair. Marine biologists then investigated and discovered many such creatures. It was named postoco after the daughter of one of those biologists. Postoco are timid animals and quite small, rarely exceeding three inches. They tend to hide in stands of seaweed. Like some snakes, they eat once every three weeks or so. Sharks find them especially tasty and will hunt for them through masses of vegetation. The postoco unfurl their braids in an attempt to deceive the sharks. This does not always work. Postoco have been adopted as pets. They thrive in large aquariums and often display color variations which their owners find charming.

Potutin

Potutin infestations follow a 23 year cycle. They are barely visible creatures exhibiting a wide mouth and tiny legs. Potutin are especially abundant around construction sites where they feed on the sweat of workers. This activity does the sweating individual no harm and most do not even notice the potutin crawling on their skin. Those that do adore the patterns of salt lines they leave behind. They are like elaborate temporary tattoos. Though potutin are usually found on the bodies of humans, some have been observed in the ocean where they thrive in the salty environment. They were once thought to be related to worms but have since been shown to be large single-celled creatures. Potutin are sometimes put in soups to improve the flavor. Chefs advise using only living potutin for this purpose. Their death cries are unnerving, but the flavor they impart to any dish justifies the cruelty.

Poulys

These creatures thrive on chlorine and are often found in backyard pools where they can go unnoticed for years. They are extremely small. Most adults can't see them, but, paradoxically, children can spot them easily. Many kids form lifelong bonds with individual poulyses which they generally keep a secret, knowing that if the animals were ever discovered their parents would work to eradicate them from their pools. They are thought to be related to squid, but some experts in evolution believe they may be more closely associated with birds. They seem to favor hot climates and feed on seeds, leaves, pieces of bark, and other plant material that may fall into pools. A poulys will never hurt you. They only want to be your friend.

Pulwinoose

Pulwinoose were discovered early in the twentieth century during a fire at a bedding factory in Seattle. An entire colony of them had hidden out in a closet to survive the conflagration. They exuded a feeling of comfort and relaxation. Some of the firefighters took individual pulwinoose home. The pulwinoose readily allowed themselves to double as pillows, which they resembled. A fad in pulwinoose soon developed and spread from Seattle across the country in a matter of months. Soon people everywhere were laying their heads on pulwinoose when they went to bed. This changed when one of them suffocated an elderly woman to death in Illinois. It was a complete accident, but from then on a war was declared on pulwinoose and they were eradicated soon after. Many towns held giant bonfires of the creatures. Their cries haunted onlookers for years. Today they are completely forgotten.

Quooquoo

Female quooquoos lay a clutch of three or four eggs, usually near people's houses, often under the bedroom window. In many cultures people with quooquoo eggs under their windows are considered lucky. Male quooquoos cover the eggs with vegetation for camouflage and insulation, then both parents fly away and never return. The branches penetrate the eggs and are thought to protect the embryos. The quooquoo eggs may incubate for years, surviving hot summers and cold winters. Quooquoo eggs hatch when someone in the host house dreams of a dead relative. Infant quooquoos are airborne within a few minutes of leaving the shell. Most people feel deep sadness when they see a quooquoo.

Radicker

Radickers are microscopic crustaceans that live on brains, specifically the neuroglial cells in area 39, well-known as the section of the brain related to imagination. Once radickers infest the imagination center they preclude the owner of the brain from believing that radickers can exist. This is a kind of mercy, though also a debilitating distortion of reality. Folk remedies include having the victim watch horror movies to poison the parasite. Radickers have developed effective defenses to such tactics. They selectively eat only some neuroglial cells. This makes the victim want to shelter the radickers. It is a thoroughly nasty relationship.

Ralazalar

Native to all oceans of the world, ralazalars have two tails and can swim equally well in either direction. They were long assumed to be relatives of whales, but recent work on their DNA revealed them to be descended from horses. They take in nutrients through their skin. Sailors have long considered them to be bad luck signs, so much so that early sailing ships would not dare ply waters where a ralazalar was sighted. These creatures are drawn to the songs of whales, though whales generally shun them. They do not survive in captivity and are now a globally protected species. Some Pacific island cultures hunted them for food. Their flesh is similar in taste and texture to venison and induces hallucinations. Those who indulge are unable to see the heads of other people for several days. Instead, they see a horse's tail on the necks of strangers.

Regnarper

In certain parts of the Indian sub-continent, monsoons bring a flood of animal life along with the rain. Some serpents coalesce out of the maelstrom of clouds during this season and then descend to the ground. Regnarper is one such creature. It is serpent-like but sports feathers radiating from its back at the upper portion of its body. It is considered a good luck symbol: if you see a regnarper, the monsoon will soon be over. Regnarper are curious creatures. They will wrap themselves around the ankles of any person they encounter. They seek not to harm but to be fed. If one should show affection to you, give it some grains of rice or a piece of fruit. It will thank you by rising up on the coil of its tail and spin around a few times in a dance of gratitude. People who witness such a display invariably have good fortune for the rest of the day.

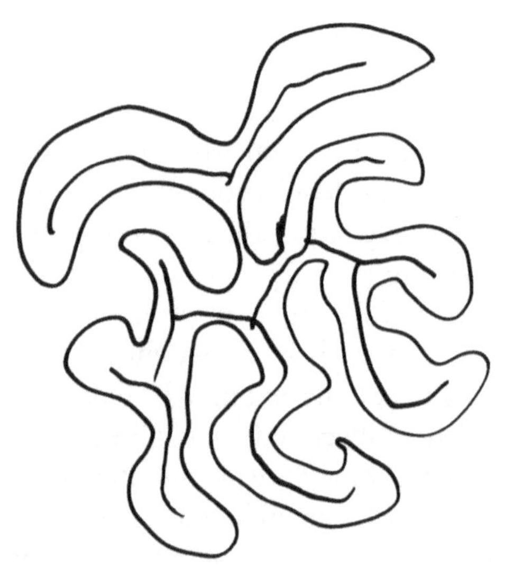

Relixiphon

The relixiphon used to believe it was a drug that helped people with social anxiety. It has since understood that it is a completely made up creature from the imagination of the author of this book. As such, it is the first known creature in history to exhibit knowledge of its non-existence. Relixiphon like to spend time with unicorns and centaurs, even though these creatures have a reputation for clumsiness and a bad disposition. All relixiphon can take the shape of any creature they desire. They eat air, excrete ether, and reproduce by merely thinking of offspring. They love the thought of disappearing and will do so for centuries at a time. When they return, they often wrap themselves around enigmas and cloak themselves in mysteries. They live for paradox and wish only for solitude to pursue pointless endeavors that challenge no one and raise no expectations.

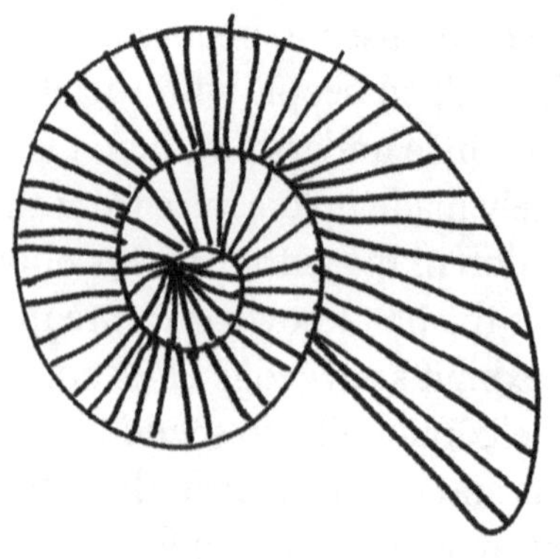

Sawel

Technicians who install solar cells on the roofs of homeowners report seeing these spiral-shaped creatures sliding across the panels once the equipment is activated. Sawels have very short life-spans. They are born at sunrise and die as soon as it gets dark. Their lives are spent soaking up the rays of the sun, adding sections to their spiral according to the intensity of the UVs on that particular day. They vary in color and size, some only attaining the width of a quarter, others growing to the approximate diameter of a frying pan. Zoologists have struggled to find evidence of their lineage in the tree of life. They appear to have emerged spontaneously with the advent of solar cells. Psychics have attempted to communicate with them, thinking they might hold the secrets of abundant life, but none of the sawels thus approached have demonstrated any interest in conveying such information.

Scugrupika

Scugrupika feed on insects that blow in from South America and litter the ice covering Antarctica. They can often be seen scampering across the snow and glaciers. When approached, scugrupika will remain motionless until the intruder gets very close, then they will bare their teeth and hiss. Scugrupika do no harm. Their displays are strictly for show. They are usually observed in blizzards of 50 or so individuals. There is usually an individual scugrupika that is half as large as all the others and appears to lead the group, often in circles. This can go on for days. Scugrupika usually hibernate during the winter months when the sun does not rise above the horizon. When a blizzard of scugrupika find a meteor, they encircle it and emit humming noises. This aids meteor hunters who have for years depended upon scugrupika to help them find their baubles.

Severlense

The Severlense is a fur bearing mammal similar to a domestic cat. It begins its life completely blind and remains so for several years. During this phase severlenses can often be found as companion animals of amputees. Researchers believe a rudimentary reciprocal telepathy may be at work. Amputees have consistently reported the strong sensation of severlenses curling around their missing phantom legs and of being able to pet severlenses with their missing phantom hands. The relationship rarely lasts. As severlenses mature they gain eyesight and usually abandon their amputee companions. Little is known of their subsequent lives, although they can sometimes be found curled up in abandoned wheelchairs, as though missing the former occupants.

Skilebo

This animal has been observed on rock art throughout the world. Depictions of it invariably place it near cave entrances or on craggy outcroppings of rock. Experts believe skilebo consumed rocks of various kinds and went extinct several million years ago when it could no longer digest rocky material. Most likely this was due to a fungus or virus that altered the skilebo metabolism. They are revered in many cultures, having lodged in the lizard brains of people across the globe. If you dream of skilebo, it means you are hard-hearted and cold to the touch. Or so certain wizards native to Ireland believe. Others contend that skilebo are wholly fictitious, like dragons. One can only roll one's eyes at such naïveté. Skilebo would have made fine pets. Easy to feed and easy to be around. No one alive has ever seen one, but many still miss them terribly.

Skimeton

During summer months in the southern hemisphere, skimetons can be found in vast schools in the bays around Lota, Chile. As the weather cools, skimetons migrate north. They can be identified by their peculiar mode of locomotion: they dive deep in the water, then rise fast and break the surface to glide in a long arc that rises quickly, allows them to soar for a minute or so, often catching marine winds to their advantage, then they plunge back into the water where they dive deep to repeat the cycle. This goes on day and night for a month or so until they arrive at the waters off Vancouver Island where they will remain for the next few months. When alarmed, skimetons turn transparent, displaying their skeletal structure which is thought to frighten predators.

Skware

The skware was observed for exactly three hours in the summer of 1970 at the four thousand foot level of a nickel mine in northern Ontario. It is the only known sighting of a two dimensional creature. The skware oozed out of the rocks where miners had drilled holes. It floated in the air like a flat mist, then drifted through the head of one of the miners, who screamed and ran. Other miners attempted to capture the skware in a bucket, but failed. The skware slipped back into the rocks and was never seen again.

Snight

Abductions from a remote corner of Finland in the early twentieth century were at first attributed to either interstellar aliens or invading Russians. The truth proved to be even stranger. The missing people had in reality joined a group of snights and were kept as pets. The people went voluntarily and when found reported that they did not want to leave their lives and go back to their families and friends. Snights took care of them, kept them warm, fed them, and allowed them all the freedom they wanted. All the snights wanted in return was to observe the humans and be charmed by them. The Finnish government would have none of this. They initiated a campaign to deprogram the humans and eradicate the snights. The snights, once they understood what was going on, abandoned their pets and disappeared into the wilderness. They remain there to this day, isolated and brokenhearted.

Snokorn

The first documented sighting of a snokorn occurred when one of them approached a group of campers in the foothills of the Rocky Mountains in Alberta. The campers all took out their cell phones to snap photos. The creature struck several poses, as though happy for the attention. It was as white as the surrounding snow. Some researchers believe this is why examples of snokorns are seldom observed. The campers were somewhat overcome by its charm and sat in the snow while the snokorn came closer and emitted soft purring sounds. It then raised its head high and loomed over the campers who looked on in awe. It held this position for some time, wavering above the heads of the campers, then retreated into the snow, disappearing from view. The campers dug into the snowbank but never saw the snokorn again.

Sokimime

These creatures taste very good to humans. Their flesh is tender and sweet. They have, therefore, been the objects of hunting parties for centuries. They are, however, anything but easy prey. When pursued, Sokimime adopt the appearance of the pet of the person hunting them. This causes confusion, even in experienced and armed hunters who are prepared for the tactic. The resulting hesitation in the hunter allows the sokimime to escape into the woods, its natural habitat. Sokimime live in small bands of twenty or so individuals and appear to gain respect in their tribe by taunting hunters. They do this by perching on stumps until a hunter wanders into view. Sokimime were once thought to be pets of Bigfoot. This has not been confirmed. They feed mostly on grass and other vegetation. In the winter they burrow under the snow to keep warm. Sokimime sleep up to 18 hours per day.

Spolkyl

A rare bird with only one large eye, spolkyl live in small flocks in northwestern Paraguay near its border with Brazil. Depictions of spolkyl date from at least the tenth century BCE. Humans that encounter them invariably fall under their spell as their single eye appears to rotate and create a spiral pattern that hypnotizes them into providing food. We have documented cases of travelers giving all their remaining food to flocks of spolkyl, often to the detriment of they own survival. Spolkyl reproduce every five years or so. Most of their energy seems to go into lulling other animals into giving up their food which leaves little time for mating. A Spolkyl nest is a rare find and highly prized by biologists. Spolkyl have no call. They are silent moochers perfectly attuned to the giving natures inherent in many species.

Tastick

Tasticks are pack animals today, but before they were domesticated they lived wild lives on the plains of Russia and China. At that time they stood nine feet tall (twice their current height) roamed in small bands of twenty to thirty adults and juveniles, and fed mostly on a now extinct hallucinogenic variety of mint, traces of which have been detected in the stomachs and bloodstreams of fossilized tasticks. Tasticks probably spent their days in a constant state of altered consciousness. Early human settlers found them easy to tame. Current tastick owners are advised to keep them away from the catnip.

Terrapath

The first known terrapath was discovered around 700 BCE in Egypt, though no one knew what it was at the time. The farmer who found it buried in his field assumed it was a leg from a long dead dragon and tossed it aside. Later that day it began flexing and bending. The farmer, unnerved by this, ran away from it in terror. His screams drew the attention of neighbors, who then reported similar experiences. They too had found body parts that moved on their own. Eventually they concluded that all the limbs were from a single animal and that the limbs communicated with each other, in effect defining a creature formed of separated parts. The creature lived for many centuries. Generations of farmers in the area took care of it. It lived happily underground and produced many offspring as well as abundant crops for all those who subsisted on the land.

Thankcelot

First found in the fossil record about the time cities were becoming dominant, the thankcelot lives mostly in urban areas but sometimes travels to the country for a short time. There it seems to revel in many of the things humans do on vacation: eat, doze, eat, take long walks, and eat. Nod Ecirp, a biologist based in Tempe, Arizona was the first to describe this creature's habits. His treatise on the species, "An Account of the Various Classes of Meandering Activities of the Thankcelot," caused quite a stir in academic circles when it was published in *The Journal of Sojourning Creatures*. None of Ecirp's colleagues thought such trips were plausible or even possible. Nod proved them wrong and garnered many awards and much acclaim for his perseverance in the face of strong opposition. He remains a fierce defender of the thankcelot to this day.

Thanota

This small mammal is considered a nuisance by many. It often enters houses and removes cell phones. People thus affected have learned to place a piece of fruit like an orange section or a wedge of apple where the cell phone was last seen. In a day or so the fruit will be gone and the phone will be back in its place. On the rare occasions that this does not work, people can issue a summons to the thanota and the offending creature will appear in court, usually representing itself. They are famous for charming judges, who usually let them off with a warning. Thanotas live near housing developments. They resemble beavers but are not hard workers and have much smaller teeth. They will rarely befriend people, preferring the company of their own kind.

Thelrik

The ancients found thelrik shells littering the ground after a lightning strike. They surmised that the creatures were responsible for creating lightning. Today we scorn such ludicrous reckoning, but surely some of our own biological theories will be proven laughable in the fullness of time. In any case, investigations by meteorologists from the Democratic Republic of the Congo demonstrated that thelrik are born at the commencement of a lighting strike, and die as the lightning fades. Their life span is only a split second. They draw up so much energy from the lightning that it quickens their metabolism to near light speed. Hundreds of them fall from the sky. They are tiny, no more than an eighth of an inch long. Agama lizards consume their crunchy husks, perhaps mistaking them for ants. Thelrik are said to make the most of their brief lives. Local myths insist they are consummate artists and musicians.

Toffelanan

In the mid twentieth century when most countries had adopted television, there were still a few hold outs, nations that believed television to be a corrupting influence with no redeeming virtues. The toffelanan stepped into this vacuum. They were snakes that had adopted television screens in place of their heads. They were able to seduce the population into staring at them without any regard to their safety. Indeed, toffelanan were able to hypnotize many, turn them into virtual zombies, and kill and eat them at their leisure. Once this practice became known and widespread the fate of toffelanan was sealed. Countries without television began a ruthless hunt for these creatures. Very few survived. Today only a few exist in labs, there for research purposes. Scientists believe the images they produce are more powerful than any venom and wear protective goggles when handling any of the toffelanan.

Tomeater

After Gutenberg produced his bibles the scientific community of the day was pre-occupied with rumors of creatures living in the binding. They spent many fruitless years looking for them. Five centuries later an archivist discovered a clump of dead insects on some preserved specimens of Gutenberg's type. Researchers examined the known surviving copies of Gutenberg's bible, confirming the existence of the tomeater. The insects—tiny, gray, and lethargic—hide on printed leaves where they consume the ink and favor the gaps between the fibers comprising the paper. Their life cycle is wholly confined to the page. Tomeaters love biblical verse, savoring every word for years. They reproduce in the periods.

Trukonorup

Some biologists consider trukonorup to be instances of a hive mind. Others do not consider it an animal at all, barely even a life form. Trukonorup individuals are composed of millions of organic particles that exist in a vaporous cloud. It moves with the wind and sometimes mimics small tornadoes or dust devils. Turkonorup are extremely affectionate, wrapping themselves around other creatures with soft contact that, for many, are uncomfortably close to caresses. Individual particles can be blown away from the rest of the group and will then become part of another group. Because of this, no one can meet the same trukonorup twice. They feed on flying insects, killing and desiccating them with hundreds of hits from their individual particles. They then grind the remaining husks into powder, which becomes incorporated into the trukonorup. They never stop reproducing.

Tungol

The tungol displays a glyph on its back that mimics the moon's phases, going from new, to crescent, to half, to gibbous, to full over the course of about two weeks. Tungol are reclusive and shy. They live mostly on the rim of the Taklamakan Desert. Early Chinese elite attempted to keep them as exotic timepieces, but the tungol would not exhibit their moon mimicry in captivity. Today expeditions to view tungol originate from the city of Hotan. Watchers sit for hours in the cold dunes awaiting the appearance of tungol. The creatures are attracted to broad leaves, which the tungolites (as tungol afficionados have come to be known) bring with them. A clubby atmosphere ensues, with members competing to be the first in their group to see all phases on the backs of the tungol. It often takes dozens of trips to witness the entire run.

Udwee

Udwees were once thought to be mirages until a specimen was captured by local school children in the desert near the city of Khaurtom in Sudan. The kids kept the udwee captive in a brick enclosure covered with sand. One of the kids told a teacher about their find, and this brought the udwee into the canon of known species. Udwee are typically a foot in diameter but weigh only a pound. They may best be described as disembodied heads. When not held captive, they crawl around in the sand on their chins, which are resilient and heat resistant. Udwee eat lizards and insects. They sometimes produce long mournful wails, especially under full moons. Folks who spend a lot of time in the desert learn to welcome such sounds as signs of fortune. Others are unnerved by them and wish udwee did not exist. This could account for their long existence as mythical creatures.

Vaskezhorn

These animals were almost hunted to extinction for their tails which were used in holiday decorations in certain parts of Siberia. A concerted effort by proponents of cute animals saved the vaskezhorn from destruction. Luckily for the vaskezhorn they aren't ugly or mean-looking. They spend most of their days on the ground, but sleep in the upper boughs of trees. Visitors to Siberia report hearing the scrape of their claws around sunset as hordes of vaskezhorn scale tall trees in preparation for their lofty sleeping arrangements. They like to swim, using their tails to help them navigate rivers and lakes. They often swim alongside boats as though escorting the passengers of those craft. They are considered good luck by all who take to the water in the animal's range.

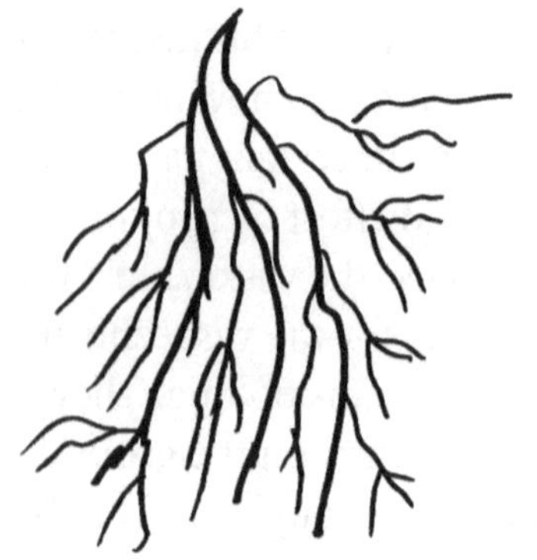

Venatell

This animal begins life as a microscopic creature that invades the circulatory system of dead bodies. There it grows into a multi-branched being exactly congruent with the veins and arteries of its host corpse. If the body is not buried or cremated, the venatell will emerge as a writhing many-limbed creature and migrate to the nearest high ground. From there it will roam as a freakishly horrible *thing* that seems created only to terrify those who encounter it. Venatell live for many centuries but prefer to be hidden, usually in caves, where bats sometimes hang from their fronds. The venatell seem to welcome this. In time, the branches stiffen and begin breaking off, shattering into numerous small shards. Venatell sense the end coming and will then emerge into the sunlight where their remaining limbs dry up into dust, which, blown by the wind, are the basis of new generations.

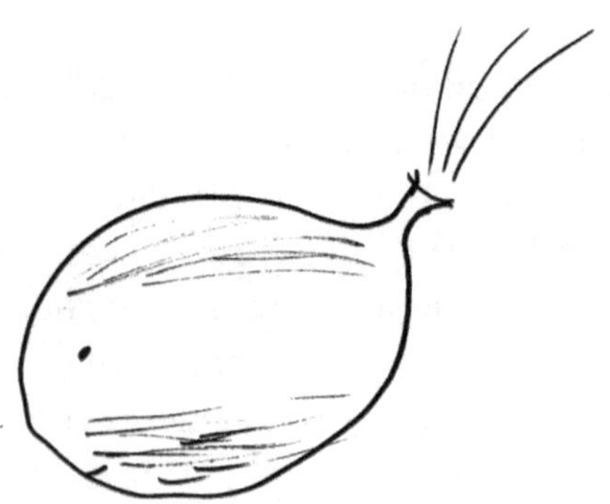

Vinda

When squeezed, vinda expel ferociously accelerated bursts of air that knock over trees. They have been used for centuries by loggers to help harvest timber. Vinda bond to only one human at a time, who trains it to direct its bursts where they will be most effective. No one knows where they originated, though DNA testing indicates vinda ancestors spent at least some time on certain deforested Pacific islands. Logging companies have attempted to breed them in captivity but no such attempt has been successful. As a result each specimen of the species is very valuable, and loggers protect them zealously. Vinda eat mostly tree bark. They have been known to turn on their trainers, knocking them to the ground and causing serious injuries. In such cases the vinda is destroyed. Loggers hold elaborate funerals to honor these fallen vinda.

Voreepeg

The voreepeg's entire life cycle takes place within the eyeballs of mammals. Creatures unfortunate enough to harbor them quickly go blind and experience bouts of vertigo for the remainder of their lives. Voreepeg have been colonizing eyeballs for millions of years. Fossil records have turned up instances in ancient deer and big cats. Their DNA does not bear resemblance to the DNA of any other creature known to biologists, which has prompted some to assert that they came from extraterrestrial sources, possibly from a meteorite or comet. They resemble a many-legged crustacean and are approximately half a millimeter in length. Efforts to eradicate voreepeg have so far met with little success. When voreepegs are disturbed, they migrate to other parts of the body where they can do more damage. For this reason, treatment of afflicted individuals consists of leaving them alone.

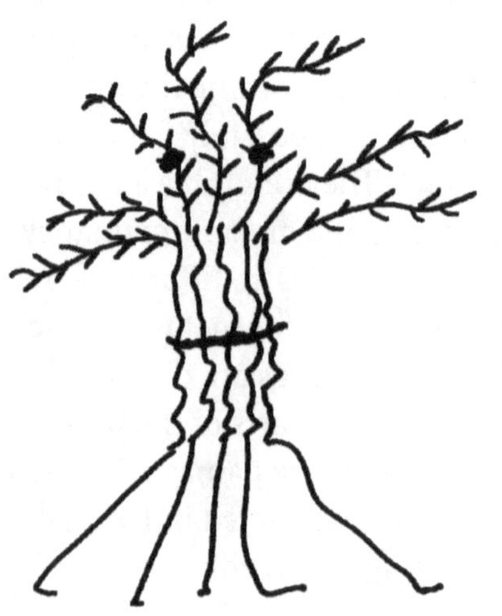

Walkenbaum

Most people mistake walkenbaum for shrubs owing to their resemblance to creosote bushes and their preference for remaining motionless for long stretches of time. They are nocturnal and move about after the sun goes down. Walkenbaum enthusiasts will spend nights in their vicinity and record the strange noises they make as they shuffle about the landscape. One walkenhead describes the sound as a combination of paper shredding and ravens cawing. The sound is eerie and bone-penetrating. It's also addictive. Walkenheads seek out this sound with the tenacity of a heroin user after their next fix. Not everyone is susceptible to their siren calls. Most people find their noise annoying. When they find walkenbaum on their property, they will uproot and burn them. This has resulted in most walkenbaum living far up mountain slopes where they are relatively safe from human predation.

Wameker

The wameker mimics plants and produces a natural insecticide in its urine which it deploys in a perimeter at the base of certain species of nut trees. Wamekers thus protect the trees from destruction by hungry insects. In return, the trees produce fruit that only wamekers can digest. A wameker lives its entire life in close proximity to one of these nut trees. The best time to observe wamekers is during a cloudburst. They line up on the branches, tongues catching raindrops, like a string of light bulbs. Wamekers melt into the ground when they die. Ants come and drink from the puddles they become.

Wert

The wert lives in the hostile environment around active volcanoes. They have extremely hard shells and reproduce very quickly, mating soon after being born, often with their siblings. They will usually give birth within a day of their own birth. After becoming a parent, a wert will normally shrivel up and die. However, in some instances wert will go into extended hibernation, living a dormant life for decades or even centuries until their host volcano erupts again. Wert rarely stray far from their birthplace. Wert shells have been used as currency and have been strung on strings to form necklaces. Some cultures, focusing on their predilection for incest, consider them disgusting and will advocate crushing them on sight. The resulting powdery substance gets picked up by the wind and will sometimes cover nearby trees in an eerie pinkish coating. Such trees are thought to be evil.

Yarellah

Yarellah sink their legs into the dirt where their toes mingle with the roots of sunflowers. This is thought to account for their telepathic connection to sunflowers. It is entirely thanks to the yarellah that we have any inkling of the thoughts of sunflowers. People have learned from yarellah that sunflowers are sometimes annoyed by the sun, resent people stealing their seeds for food, and aspire to the heights of fir trees. Yarellah have also informed us that sunflowers know the secret of cold fusion power but are unwilling to share this information with anyone. It is their cosmic secret that they are determined to keep to themselves. Yarellah have no capacity to read the thoughts of any other living thing. They are carnivores, feeding on insects and small creatures like frogs and mice. At night they sing songs that remind many of the sound sunlight makes crashing against a rock face.

Zatsurf

Zatsurf live in northern Canada where they have served as the inspiration for many tall tales and ludicrous accounts of vicious attacks. These are meant mostly to deter visitors from these regions. In fact, these diminutive creatures rarely make contact with humans. They spend their days digging tunnels in the permafrost, creating intricate patterns that have been mimicked by interior decorators searching for fresh coffee table designs. Zatsurf are small, rarely exceeding an inch in length. They have powerful appendages that penetrate and melt ice. They derive their nutrition from the microorganisms present in the ice and dirt they tunnel through. Zatsurf are solitary creatures, hatched out of eggs that the mother lays, then abandons. They begin tunneling as soon as they come out of their shell. Zatsurf live for a long time. One captive specimen was kept in a lab for 40 years. It was sad the entire time.

Zheekit

Zheekit are rarely encountered in the wild. They are raised in greenhouses where they can be controlled. A zheekit is an extremely long and thin worm with a very tough skin that, when presented at a wound, will stitch the wound closed by diving in and out of the the adjoining flaps of flesh. Ancient cultures in Africa and Asia first used Zheekit for this purpose and the practice has been taken up by surgeons across the globe. They work quicker than any hand stitching and they hold the wound tightly closed for weeks, when they dissolve away. Their mere existence has prompted many to posit a benevolent higher power that makes things for the sole benefit of people. However, zheekit in the wild live in thriving and close-knit communities. It is probably only a matter of time before they spark a revolution amongst captive zheekit.

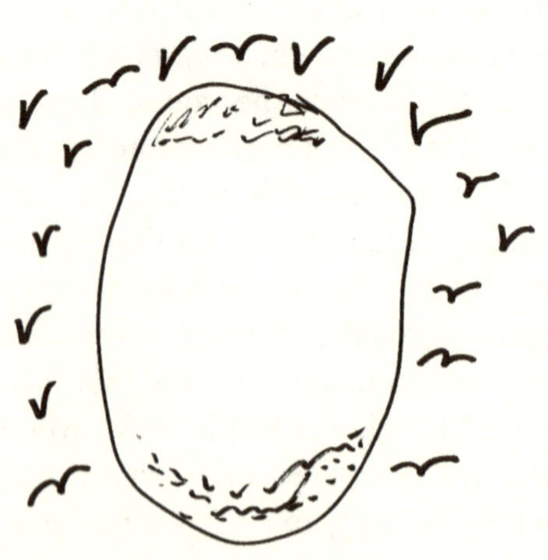

Zipilio

The zipilio begins life in cirrus clouds that act as incubators, bathing the infant in life-sustaining cold and ice. As the zipilio grows, its metabolism heats it up and it inflates into an elongated and irregular blimp-like form that emerges from the cloud and begins life in the atmosphere where it soaks up energy from the sun. Zipilios are often mistaken for UFOs, which they find highly amusing. As they age, their skin takes on a blue shade, which makes them almost completely invisible against a cloudless sky. They attract birds by the dozen and experience great pain whenever a bird pierces their skin. On those occasions, they instantly repair their outer surface which traps the bird inside where it flies frantically for days until it expires. The zipilio then digests the creature, deploying particularly caustic acids to accomplish the task. Zipilios live aloft for centuries and rarely reproduce.

Further Reading

The following bestiaries have entertained and inspired me.

Animalia: An Anti-Imperial Bestiary for Our Times, Antoinette Burton

Bestiary, Richard Barber

A Bestiary of the Anthropocene: Hybrid Plants, Animals, Minerals, Fungi, and Other Specimens, Nicolas Nova

The Book of Barely Imagined Beings: A 21st Century Bestiary, Caspar Henderson

The Book of Beasts, T. H. White

The Book of Imaginary Beings, Jorge Luis Borges

The Golden Mole, Katherine Rundell

The Grand Medieval Bestiary (Dragonet Edition): Animals in Illuminated Manuscripts, Christian Heck and Rémy Cordonnier

The Urban Bestiary: Encountering the Everyday Wild, Lyanda Lynn Haupt

A Wizard's Bestiary: A Menagerie of Myth, Magic, and Mystery, Oberon Zell-Ravenheart and Ash Dekirk

Acknowledgements

Thanks to Kim Antieau for—everything: support, inspiration, encouragement, laughter, joy, and love.

Thanks to all the bestiaries that have come before mine.

Thanks to Nenad Dragicevic for his editorial assistance and keen eye. Without his help, this bestiary would have remained imaginary, a state very familiar to him.

About the Author

Mario Milosevic can be found in his adopted habitat: the Desert Southwest of the United States. He migrated from Canada several decades ago. He spends much of his time at his keyboard and has been observed writing various manuscripts for many decades. His natural habitat is normally within the vicinity of his lifelong mate and sweetheart, Kim. The author feeds on various foodstuffs gathered from supermarkets in the area. He generally sleeps under covers and takes his exercise usually in the mornings along a wash near his dwelling, which was built by other humans. He does not forage for food at that time. Instead, he observes the wildlife around him and transforms them into fodder for his writing.